Night Lights

Steven Schnur

Pictures by **Stacey Schuett**

Frances Foster Books • Farrar Straus Giroux • New York

Library of Congress Cataloging-in-Publication Data

Schnur, Steven.

Night lights / Steven Schnur ; pictures by Stacey Schuett. — 1st ed.

p. cm.

Summary: Each night before going to bed, Melinda counts the lights, from
one seashell on the nursery wall to a million twinkling stars.

ISBN 0-374-35522-3

[1. Counting. 2. Night—Fiction. 3. Bedtime—Fiction. 4. Stories in rhyme.]
I. Schuett, Stacey, ill. II. Title.

PZ8.3.S2973Ni   2000

[E]—dc21   99-22386

For Juliana

My cherished day and night light

—Steven Schnur

For Mark, Beth, and Fiona

—Stacey Schuett

Each night before she goes to bed,
Melinda counts the lights:

ONE seashell on the nursery wall,

TWO blinking amber clocks,

THREE burning logs within the grate,
FOUR candles near the blocks.

FIVE TV sets across the street,
SIX lanterns on the lawn,

And SEVEN blinking fireflies,

EIGHT windows, lit till dawn.

NINE pairs of gleaming raccoon eyes,
TEN flashlights sweep the sky,

ELEVEN racing bicycles,

TWELVE headlights rumble by.

THIRTEEN streetlamps light the park,
FOURTEEN stoplights blink,

FIFTEEN towers scrape the sky,
SIXTEEN bridges wink.

SEVENTEEN beacons sweep the coast,
EIGHTEEN ships untie,

NINETEEN train cars light the tracks,
TWENTY airplanes fly.

FIFTY pond-reflected moons,

ONE HUNDRED lightning bars,

A THOUSAND

sparkling fireworks,

ONE MILLION twinkling stars!